This book belongs to:

....

For my Thea Pearl.

In loving memory of Cindy, Peter & Dean.

I know you're feeling sad my dear,
I know your heart is feeling down.
But I need to tell you a secret,
to ease that weary frown.

You see, my dear, they didn't just go,
you're just not seeing enough.
Lift your head, my darling,
look up when it feels tough.

They are there, up in the air.

I promise, it's not always this rough.

I know, when someone goes away,
who you love with your whole heart.
It feels like nothing will be the same,
and you don't know where to start.

But when they go, they're not just gone,
they are free and in the sky.
If you lift your head and take a breath,
and widen those beautiful eyes.

You will see them far away,
BOLDER and BRIGHTER than ever.

Shining down and watching you,
as a BRAND NEW STAR, forever.

If your head is low and you wear a frown,
you won't notice what they send.
Like a warm breeze or a tiny feather,
to show you this is not the end.

Sometimes it's the sunshine,
or maybe a ladybird.
It could even be a feeling,
or a nice song that you heard.

They will want you to be happy,
to still sing your happy songs.
Be sad if you need to, it's ok,
but please, don't dwell for too long.

These things will be around you,
they won't always feel so bad.
A time will come, when you will smile,
for all the good times that you had.

Remember all they taught you,
and all the love you shared.
Look out for those feathers,
and the warm breeze in the air.

They are there and they still love you,
that can never go away.
Keep your memories in your heart,
and there, they will always stay.

Acknowledgements

My Dale, thank you for always supporting my dreams and wild ideas, for the endless proof-reading and brutally honest, but extremely helpful critique.
For always being fully aboard my crazy train, no matter how rocky it gets!
I love and appreciate you more than any words could express.
My wonderful daughter, Megan. Your self-belief and determination have always been inspiring to everyone around you, especially me. Thank you for your influence and honesty.
My lovely son, Max. Thank you for your never-ending humour and
love and showing me that absolutely anything can be funny.
My little ray of sunshine, Thea. Thank you for getting me through some of my darkest days with your constant joyfulness and kindness.
These books will forever be yours.

To my amazing friends and family. From the bottom of my rusty old heart, thank you for your relentless encouragement, patience, and support,
I will never forget it.

Dedication

My incredible Ma, Cindy. Thank you for always teaching me to express myself through art and how to take something positive from a bad situation. Thank you for the signs you send me. I will always look for them.
Pete, Thank you for your constant guidance, advice, support, and belief. I would love nothing more than to be able to deliver you this book you so wanted me to write. Wherever you are,
I hope it's still a funny old world, kid.
My friend, Dean. The thirst you had for life keeps me going every day. Thank you for always being such a great friend.

-See you on the next star.

Love always, Gem.